A HAPPY ENDING BOOK ™

the Flyaway Kite

by Jane Carruth   illustrated by

MODERN PUBLISHING
A Division of Unisystems, In

New York, New York 10022

Printed in Belgium

Hoppity always wanted to do the same things as his brother Bobtail. One day Bobtail was flying his kite. Hoppity cried, "Let me try."

He tugged the string out of Bobtail's hand. The kite
flew away and landed in a tall tree.
"Now look what you have done!" said Bobtail.

Hoppity tried to climb up the tree
to get the kite. But he forgot that he
was wearing his new pants. Soon he
tore a big hole in them.

Back at home, Mommy and Daddy quickly found out
what had happened, and they were angry with
Hoppity. "What a bad boy you are," said Daddy.
"You better go straight to bed!"

Sadly Hoppity tucked himself in bed, and soon he
was fast asleep. Then he began to dream of kites.
Lots of brightly colored kites, with faces, seemed
to be chasing him. Some of them seemed to be
laughing at him, others looked angry or sad.
Hoppity ran away from them as fast as he could.
"Help me! Help me!" he cried aloud.

As he woke up suddenly, he was glad
to see Mommy and Daddy standing by
the bed. Even sleepy Bobtail had
come to comfort Hoppity.
"Don't be scared," said Mommy. "We
will stay with you, and you will soon
forget your bad dream."

Hoppity soon fell asleep again, and in the morning
he felt much better. After breakfast, Bobtail left
for school. Hoppity and his mother waved goodbye
to him at the door.

Hoppity went back to the tree, but the kite was out of reach. "Never mind," said a little bird, "I know how we can get it down for you!"

In a minute Tim Squirrel, and many more little birds,
came and rescued the kite.
"Thank you very much," called Hoppity, and he ran
home with the flyaway kite under his arm.

"Look, Mommy, I've got the kite back!" he called.
But then he saw that it was torn, and had lost some
of its beautiful tail.
"Oh, dear, it's all broken," he said sadly.

Mommy had a look at the torn kite.
"That's not so bad," she smiled. "We can make
it strong enough to fly again!"
Out came her sewing box and she sewed a neat
patch over the hole. Hoppity sat down and made
a lovely new tail to flutter behind the kite.

The day passed very quickly, and soon Bobtail came home from school. Hoppity was very glad to see his brother. "Here's your kite," he smiled. "And it's just as good as new."
Bobtail was so pleased he gave Hoppity a hug.

Hoppity had another surprise for his brother.
"Look!" he cried proudly. "Mommy mended my
torn pants and put a patch on them, and it's just the
same shape as your kite. So now I've got a kite
of my own!"

"Perhaps we can do even better than that," said
Bobtail with a wink. He didn't tell Hoppity what
he meant, but a few days later there was a lovely
surprise for Hoppity on his birthday—a new
kite, just like Bobtail's!
"Let's go and fly them together," cried Hoppity.
As they ran along, the little birds who had
rescued the flyaway kite joined in the fun.